Broomstick Removals

salute you, noble brooms,
Rise and fly around these rooms."

Still nothing happened.

"You're hopeless, you two. Here, let me have
a go," said Maud eagerly, her eyes flashing as in
the old days. Black Cat ran over to her, purring
loudly with delight.

"By toad in ditch and owl in tree,
Brooms, you'd better fly for me.
If you don't, you'll meet a fate,
That I think you both would hate!"

Also by Ann Jungman

Broomstick Baby
Broomstick Rescues
Broomstick Services

Septimouse, Supermouse!
Septimouse, Big Cheese!
Septimouse and the Cheese Party

Ann Jungman

Broomstick Removals

Illustrated by
Jan Lewis

Happy Cat Books

For Audrey with love

HAPPY CAT BOOKS

Published by Happy Cat Books Ltd.
Bradfield, Essex CO11 2UT, UK

This edition published 2004
1 3 5 7 9 10 8 6 4 2

Copyright © Ann Jungman, 1997
Illustrations copyright © Jan Lewis, 1997
The moral rights of the author and illustrator have been asserted
All rights reserved

A CIP catalogue record for this book is available from the British Library

ISBN   1 903285 72 0

Printed in Poland

Chapter 1

A New Customer

Ethel picked up the phone for the thirtieth time that night. "Broomstick Services here. How can I help you? Seven fish and chips, with pickled onions and gherkins? Fine, Mrs O'Malley, we'll deliver them to you within ten minutes. Number 141 on the fourteenth floor, isn't it? Now be waiting at your window and my sister will deliver your food all piping hot. Thank you Mrs O'Malley, it's a pleasure. Enjoy your meal. Byee!"

"This is the thirtieth delivery tonight," moaned Mabel. "I'm exhausted, it's started to rain, and we only earn peanuts. There must be an easier way to make a living! I'm fed up."

"We'll make this the last order tonight," Ethel promised her. "Now off you go and I'll have a nice hot cup of cocoa waiting when you get back."

So Mabel flew off down to the fish and chip shop, then over to 141 to deliver, and finally back home to fall asleep by the fire with Ethel and Black Cat.

The following morning they were all still sleeping deeply when there was a loud ring at the door. Mabel woke up with a start and her hat fell on to the floor. Picking the hat up with one hand and grabbing the phone with the other, she signalled to her sister.

"Coming," yelled Ethel, as she raced around, opening the curtains and kicking the cups behind the chairs. Black Cat fled, miaowing. "Keep on talking, Mabel, we don't want whoever it is to think that we're not very busy indeed."

"I know," agreed her sister. "Not good for our image, not good for business."

After a quick look round to check everything was in place, Ethel opened the door. She returned a minute later followed by a very plump, bald, worried-looking man. Mabel nodded to him and continued with her pretend telephone conversation. "We're very busy at the moment, very, very busy, you'll have to wait at least six months, I'm afraid. Yes, ring back in six months, that will be best." Then she put the phone down and faced the man. She noted that he looked very worried indeed. "Now, sir," she said, "why don't you sit down and tell us what we can do for you?"

"Well, not very much, I'm afraid – I heard you saying on the phone that you were busy

for the next six months!"

"Well, er, yes," said Mabel. "But we can always fit in someone with a nice face. Isn't that right, Ethel?"

"Definitely," agreed her sister. "Oh, definitely, we would see it as our duty."

"You are so kind," said the man gratefully, and he managed a small smile.

"So," said Mabel. "Come on, out with it. What's your problem and how can we help?"

"It's so difficult to know where to start," mumbled the man.

"At the beginning might be a good place," suggested Mabel helpfully.

"Well, my name is Botch, er, Barnaby Botch of Botch, Bungle and Break Builders."

The two witches tried hard not to giggle. "How do you do, Mr Botch?" said Mabel, with an almost straight face. "I'm Mabel and this is Ethel, my sister."

The man nodded, sat down miserably in a chair and looked at the floor.

"Come on, Mr Botch," said Ethel kindly. "You can tell us what the problem is, we're used to solving problems."

"It's just that every morning when I arrive at my builder's yard, I find it full of rubbish, and me and Bill Bungle and Bertie Break have to spend hours packing it up and taking it off to the tip. Frankly we're sick of it, and we were hoping you would help."

"Sounds like you need to go to the police," commented Ethel.

"We're rather anxious not to do that," said Mr Botch, coughing and going a bit red. "It doesn't do a business any good if the police get involved."

"Well, I don't see how we could help," declared Mabel. "We're a delivery service, not a rubbish disposal business."

"I see," said Mr Botch, looking very downcast. "You were my last hope, but I didn't think you'd be able to do anything." Then he got up and walked gloomily to the door.

He looked so sad a tear ran down Ethel's face.

"Don't despair, Mr Botch," she cried. "We may be able to do something. We'll sleep on it and get back to you tomorrow."

"Come on, Ethel, not so fast. We're not in the rubbish disposal business," cried her sister. "We don't have the right equipment – I wouldn't know where to start – and we'd have to get up very, very early in the morning!"

"Well, I like a new challenge," said Ethel

firmly. "And you know what they say, 'Early to bed and early to rise, makes a witch healthy and wealthy and wise'."

"We'll get back to you tomorrow morning first thing," said Mabel, opening the door for Mr Botch. "Thank you for coming, Mr Botch, nice to meet you."

As soon as the door closed she rounded on

Ethel. "Whatever got into you, Ethel? We don't want a job like that!"

"*I* do," replied her sister defiantly. "I'm bored of just delivering food. I'm ready for a big new challenge and I liked poor Mr Botch *and* we need money for a few things around the house."

"Like what?" demanded Mabel.

"We need a tumble-dryer and a video recorder."

"That's true," agreed Mabel. "And I would like a microwave too."

"And if we do this job we can charge more than we can for delivering food," Ethel pointed out.

"I see," nodded Mabel. "I begin to follow your train of thought, Ethel, and I agree Mr Botch did look so miserable. I think we should agree to help him."

"So we could kill two birds with one stone," said Mabel. "Earn a bit of extra money and do a good deed."

"My point exactly," nodded Ethel.

"And if we have to get up early in the morning," said Mabel, "and work till late at night, our siesta in the middle of the day will be even more important."

"It will, it will," agreed Ethel.

"Well, tomorrow morning will be our first crack-of-dawn morning," Mabel pointed out, "so we'd better get on with our siesta now, or we'll be in no kind of shape tomorrow morning."

So Ethel took the phone off the hook and put a notice on the door saying

BROOMSTICK SERVICES
CLOSED 'till 6 P.M.
DO NOT DISTURB!
(serious sleeping
is taking place.)

and they both went back to sleep.

That evening before they started their nightly deliveries of food, Ethel rang Mr Botch to tell him that they had decided to take the job. "It will be a new challenge for us," she told him, "and we think we should always do a good deed if we can – it's part of the Modern Witch's Charter."

Mr Botch was delighted. "Oh, Miss Mabel, Miss Ethel, I am so grateful. Just wait till I tell Billy Bungle and Bertie Break, they'll go mad with joy. Would it be too much to ask you to start tomorrow?"

"It will be a pleasure," Ethel told him. "We'll be there at 5 a.m., on the dot!"

Chapter 2

Garbage

At 4.30 a.m. the next day, the alarm clock went off.

"Turn the wretched thing off, Ethel," said Mabel grumpily, and she turned over to go back to sleep.

"Come on, Mabel," declared Ethel firmly. "Up you get! Remember we're going to clear away all that disgusting rubbish from poor Mr Botch's building yard."

"Changed my mind," muttered Mabel, and went straight back to sleep.

Ethel shook Mabel again and again but only got the reply, "Go 'way, leave me 'lone."

"Huh," sniffed Ethel indignantly. Then she went and got a jug of cold water and poured it over Mabel's head.

Mabel sat up in bed and glared at her sister. "Have you finally gone completely mad, Ethel?" she yelled.

"Well, you wouldn't wake up," Ethel pointed out, "and we have to go and move the rubbish as we agreed."

"Wish I never had," grumbled Mabel, as she struggled into her clothes.

"Tell you what, Mabel, I'll treat you to a full cooked breakfast once we've finished, over at Giovanni's Cafe."

Mabel grinned. "You have got yourself a deal," she declared.

So shortly after, the two witches and Black Cat flew over the fence of the building yard, each holding one handle of the biggest plastic laundry bag they could find. They landed in the yard and looked with horror at the huge pile of rubbish. There were empty tin cans, rotting fruit and vegetables, an old pram, punctured tyres, disposable nappies, broken bottles, a mattress with the springs coming out and a load of broken eggs.

"Gosh, doesn't it stink?" complained Mabel, holding her nose.

"Yes, and isn't there a lot of it!" agreed her sister.

"Miaow!" said Black Cat firmly and with his tail straight up in the air, he stomped off and disappeared over the fence.

"Oh dear, maybe this job wasn't such a good

idea after all," moaned Mabel.

"Just think about that lovely video recorder, my dear," replied Ethel, "and about what a good deed we are doing, and of that delicious, hot, full English breakfast I promised you."

"Okay, but we'd better go and get some rubber gloves," grumbled Mabel.

"It's disgusting, just dumping all that stuff in poor Mr Botch's yard."

"It jolly well is," agreed Ethel. "You're right about the gloves, and we may as well get a couple of face masks and some pegs for our noses, while we're at it."

So the witches returned a bit later wearing big red washing-up gloves, masks to cover their mouths, and pegs on their noses. As fast as they could, they shovelled the rubbish into the laundry bag and flew it over to the municipal dump.

"We must be very careful not to spill any," Ethel reminded Mabel. "If this stuff started to fall on people there would be no end of trouble."

"I know," agreed Mabel, giggling. "No joke if it rained rotten potato peel or soggy peas."

"Yes, or old tins of cat food," sniggered Ethel.

So they flew slowly and carefully to the municipal dump no less than five times. The job was finished just as everyone else was getting up and having breakfast. As they flew back to their flat on the thirty-fifth floor, smells of frying bacon wafted up from an open window.

"I'm starving," announced Mabel. "Let's go straight and have that cooked breakfast you promised me at Giovanni's Cafe."

"Good idea," agreed her sister. "That job was hard work – I'm a bit hungry myself! "

So the two witches swooped down and

landed in the car park of the cafe and went in, clutching their broomsticks. At the tables sat men in work clothes eating huge plates of egg, bacon, sausages, tomato, mushrooms and fried bread, sipping piping hot tea from big mugs and munching away on crispy toast.

Mabel and Ethel knew most of them and

waved enthusiastically as they entered.

"Morning all," cried Mabel. "Two full English breakfasts, Giovanni, and look sharp about it – we're starving."

"Cor, what a pong," yelled someone. "I'm out of here."

"You two stink something terrible," said another. "We're trying to eat in here, you know!"

Giovanni came running out of the kitchen. "Miss Mabel, Miss Ethel, what are you trying to do to my business? You are trying to ruin me?"

"No, Giovanni, all we want is some breakfast."

"I will give you breakfast, happily, I will give you ten breakfasts, but only after you have washed and changed."

"Do we smell that bad?" asked the witches in a surprised tone.

"You stink," Giovanni told the firmly. "Now out of my cafe and into the bath I think."

Miserably the witches got on to their broomsticks and flew home. When they got there, their older sister Maud and their good friend Jackie were waiting for them.

"I had a phone call from Giovanni," Maud told them, holding a scented white hankie up to her nose. "The bath is ready – I've put a whole package of bath salts in it. Now strip those stinking clothes off as quickly as you can."

While the sisters were bathing, Jackie quickly shoved all the clothes in the washing-machine and slammed the door on them.

"Wash your hair thoroughly as well," Maud shouted sternly from outside the bathroom door. "I want you two smelling as fresh as daisies in spring when you come out."

Eventually, Ethel and Mabel emerged from the bathroom, their hair dripping, and wearing their other set of witch clothes.

"I am absolutely starving," moaned Mabel. "Ethel promised me a full English breakfast."

"Well, I'm not having you going out with

wet hair," declared Maud firmly. "I mean, what would the neighbours think? To say nothing of the dangers of catching a chill."

"I'll die if I don't get breakfast soon," complained Mabel, on the verge of tears.

"Maud, why don't you take one of the broomsticks and go over to Giovanni's and get two breakfasts and fly back with them?" suggested Jackie.

"Don't be silly, dear," said Maud tartly.

"You know perfectly well that I gave up witchcraft when I married your uncle, my darling Fred."

"Couldn't you do it just this once?" suggested Jackie. "I mean, this is a bit of an emergency."

"Never!" declared Maud dramatically. "I have forsworn witchery."

"I think you're just scared," said Ethel. "And out of practice. I don't believe you could carry two plates of hot food and two big mugs of scalding tea this high any more."

"How dare you suggest that I've lost my skills!" shrieked Maud, her eyes flashing. "Or that I, Maud, daughter of the Great Witch

Foxglove and granddaughter of the Witch of Witches Merlina cannot make magic whenever or wherever I please. Hand me a broomstick, Jackie, and I'll show you all my undiminished skills." And Maud leapt on to the broomstick and flew away.

"Hah, she fell straight into that one," said Ethel, laughing. Mabel and Jackie giggled too.

"Get the knives and forks out, Jackie," said Mabel through the towel with which she was drying her hair. "Not a moment to waste."

Within five minutes, Maud was back, carrying two fried breakfasts, four slices of toast, butter, marmalade and two huge mugs of tea on a tray. "There you are Ethel, I have lost none of my skill and none of my nerve. You owe me an apology."

Ethel was greedily munching a piece of toast. "I admit I was wrong, Maud. You are as good a witch as ever you were and you can fly faster than either Mabel or me. Isn't that right, Mabel?"

Mabel had her mouth full, but nodded enthusiastically in agreement and then went on eating her breakfast.

The next day the witches had to deliver six loads of rubbish to the dump and on the day after, seven.

"We should call ourselves Broomstick Removals," grumbled Mabel.

"I know," agreed Ethel, leaning on her broomstick and rubbing the sweat off her brow. "I don't know how long I can go on doing this day after day, Mabel, it gets more each morning."

"And each day we have to wait longer for our breakfast," moaned Mabel.

"I could just do with a little sleep," yawned Ethel.

"Why don't we do that? No one would

know," said Mabel. "Just five minutes before we take the last lot to the dump."

So the witches left their broomsticks by the bag of rubbish and went up the steps into Mr Botch's office, to get away from the smell. They slept and slept until they were woken by Mr Botch's voice.

"Miss Mabel, Miss Ethel, wake up – it's nine o'clock."

The two witches sat up suddenly. Mr Botch put his hankie to his nose, and said, "I don't know quite what to say to you two. I mean, there's still one bag of rubbish left downstairs."

"Don't you worry, Mr Botch," Mabel assured him. "My sister and I will take it straight to the dump and then head for home."

The witches stumbled down the stairs and looked around for the broomsticks. They were nowhere to be seen.

"Hey? Mr Botch," yelled Mabel. "Have you seen our broomsticks? Did you put them somewhere?"

Mr Botch stuck his head out of the window, looking worried. "I didn't touch them. Hang on a minute, I'll give old Bill Bungle a shout, he may know. Bill, our rubbish removal service can't find their broomsticks. Did you take them?"

A jolly man with a load of red hair stuck his head out of a top-floor window.

"That's a silly question, Barnaby. What would I want with a broomstick? You know

I get air sick. Give old Bertie a ring, he may know."

So Mr Botch rang Bertie Break, who came running up. He was very tall and thin and bespectacled.

"Oh dear, oh dear," said Mr Break, shaking his head and biting his lip. "I'm afraid I haven't seen a thing, I've been buried in the accounts since eight o'clock this morning. This is bad news, oh dear, oh dear. Whatever next? I ask myself."

"Where did you see the broomsticks last?" asked Mr Botch.

"Just here by the rubbish," Mabel told him in an anxious tone.

"They've gone," whimpered Ethel, looking scared.

"Oh, no!" cried Mabel, tears rolling down her plump cheeks. "How will we manage? How will we run Broomstick Services? What will we tell Maud? Oh, Ethel, this is a disaster!"

Chapter 3

Rivals

"What are we going to do?" asked Ethel, looking at her sister desperately. "We've lost our precious broomsticks." A tear ran down her cheek. "Now we can't even get home."

"I know, I know," mumbled Mabel gloomily. "Maybe we should phone the police."

"Oh, I wouldn't do that yet," said Mr Botch, sounding a little worried. "I mean, the brooms are probably just mislaid. The minute you're not looking for them they'll turn up. And I promise to phone you the moment they do."

"Well, all right," agreed Mabel, with a big sigh. "Come on Ethel, we'd better get going."

"I'm too tired to walk," moaned her sister. "Let's take a bus."

"We can't do that – the bus driver would

never let us get on."

"That's true," grumbled Ethel. "Then let's treat ourselves and call a taxi."

"No cabbie would let you get into his cab smelling like that," Mr Botch pointed out.

"You just watch it, Botch," snapped Mabel. "This is all your fault. I knew this job was a mistake. If it wasn't for your soft heart, Ethel, all that helping the community and the locals and playing our part and everything, we wouldn't be standing here now, smelly and starving and no way of getting home."

"Maud!" said Ethel in a loud voice.

"Yes, that's what we'll have to do. We'll bite on the bullet and phone Maud and get her to collect us. She never got rid of her broom, you know. She keeps it in the wardrobe."

"But even if she agreed, she'd keep us waiting for ages," moaned Mabel. "And we'd never hear the end of it. I'd rather just sit here and wait."

"Not possible I'm afraid, ladies," said Mr Botch politely, looking at his watch.

"My workmen will be arriving soon and your

odour, well, it will be a bit rich for them too."

"Maybe we could cover up our faces and run through the streets and then race into the estate and into our own block, up in the lift and up to the thirty-fifth floor and no one would be any the wiser. What do you say, Ethel?"

"No, everyone would know it was us, Mabel," replied Ethel. "And anyway you're too big to run fast and we're both out of practice."

Mabel nodded grimly. "Do you have Maud's phone number on you?"

"I can remember it," Ethel told her sister

proudly. "I'll go and call her now."

"Please don't touch anything while you're down there," said Mr Botch, going a bit red. "Sorry, but the smell you know."

Ethel came up the stairs a few minutes later, looking very down in the mouth.

"Isn't she coming?" asked her sister.

"Oh, she's coming all right, on her broomstick, straight away – but she sounded very cross."

Five minutes later there was a rush of wind and Maud flew angrily round the builder's yard five times before she landed.

"I don't know, really I do not know," she announced loudly as she got off her broom. "I was just waving goodbye to my darling Fred and getting ready to do my washing when I got your call. You both know that I am retired but you will keep doing the daftest things and dragging me back in with the two of you."

"Sorry, Maud," mumbled Mabel, in a small voice.

"We tried to think of every other way of getting home before we called you, Maud," Ethel told her.

"Well, next time something goes wrong you are on your own, do you understand that? You two bird-brained apologies for witches! This is the last time I help you, is that clear?"

"Yes, Maud," they chorused together.

"And where is Black Cat, pray?"

"He, er, well actually he didn't like the smell," confessed Ethel.

"Well I don't blame him! Now up on to my broomstick and let's just hope it can take the weight of all three of us.

We'll fly straight to my flat and you can bath and change. I just hope we can get in there unnoticed, I'd hate the neighbours to know about this! Now say thank you to Mr Botch and apologize for all the trouble you've caused him and we'll be off."

As soon as the two were washed and changed Maud said: "Well, now you'd better telephone the police and report a certain theft."

Nervously Mabel picked up the phone and rang the police station. The police were very sympathetic but said they didn't think they'd be able to help, as one broomstick looked much like another, but that if anyone handed a broomstick in to Lost Property, they would definitely be in touch.

Mabel and Ethel sat miserably on the couch in Maud's sparkling neat front room. "How are we going to run Broomstick Services tonight?" asked Ethel gloomily.

"We can't do it," sighed Mabel.

"Oh, you two make me sick," snapped Maud. "We'll just go to the market and buy a couple of new brooms, you unimaginative pair of quitters."

"But Maud," said Mabel patiently, "you know that we've almost forgotten our magic."

"Yes, I do remember that, sisters mine, but I have an excellent memory and between us

I'm sure we can magic the new brooms into splendid witches' broomsticks. In fact, we'll use the same magic you once used to magic two squeegy mops, if I remember rightly. I may be retired but I am still of sound mind, to say nothing of very determined. Now come along, you two, to the market let us go without delay!"

An hour later they returned home, clutching two brand new brooms. "All right, do your stuff, Maud," said Mabel, grinning. "I can't wait to see."

"Have a go yourselves, you lazy good-for-nothings," snapped Maud.

So Ethel raised her hands in the air. Suddenly, Black Cat raced out of the kitchen and sat on her shoulder. Then Ethel chanted:

"Broomsticks, broomsticks from our market fair,
Rise, rise, rise into the air."

Nothing happened.

"Here, let me try," said Mabel, rolling up her sleeves and spitting on her hands. Black Cat went and sat on her shoulder and wailed noisily in encouragement.

"We salute you noble brooms,
Rise and fly around these rooms."

Still nothing happened.

"We've lost our touch, no two ways about it," moaned Mabel.

"You're hopeless, you two. Here, let me have

a go," said Maud eagerly, her eyes flashing as in the old days. Black Cat ran over to her, purring loudly with delight.

"By toad in ditch and owl in tree,
Brooms, you'd better fly for me.
If you don't, you'll meet a fate,
That I think you both would hate!"

Black Cat let out a big caterwaul and the two brooms flew round the room. Maud grinned and rubbed her hands together.

"Oh, well done, Maud!" cried Ethel. "You always were the best."

"The very, very best!" agreed Mabel.

"You just have to let them know who is boss," said Maud in a pleased tone. "Well, sisters, I seem to have solved all your problems."

Just then there was a loud, continuous ring at the door.

"Someone's in a big hurry," commented Ethel.

Maud flung open the door and there stood Jackie, looking very upset and clutching a batch of flyers.

"It is NOT necessary to lean on the bell like that," said Maud fiercely.

"Yes it is, it is!" cried Jackie. "Look at these! Everyone has got one. What are you going to do?"

The witches looked at the papers Jackie handed them. On them was written:

BROOMSTICK DELIVERIES
Your cheapest ever fast food delivery service!
ONCE USED, NEVER FORGOTTEN!
Half the price of any other delivery service and twice as hot.
Be at your window tonight to see the newest, most up-to-date delivery service known to man...'BROOMSTICK DELIVERIES'
Wham, Bam, Zow!
Forget 'Broomstick Services' and use us and get a free Coke with each delivery. Get your food, HOTTER, FASTER, TASTIER, and CHEAPER, with the people's delivery service...
BROOMSTICK DELIVERIES

"Oh, dear," said Ethel. "Whatever will we do? No one will want Broomstick Services any more."

"I know," agreed Mabel sadly. "We're finished – they're much cheaper than us."

"What will you do?" asked Jackie.

"I don't know," sighed Ethel.

"It's not fair!" Jackie wept. "We thought of Broomstick Services and now they're muscling in on our act."

"Well, sisters, you certainly have made a mess of things," thundered Maud. "You let some creep steal your broomsticks and now you're in deep trouble and this time I'm not at all sure I'm in the mood to help you."

Chapter 4

The Villains

That night Ethel and Mabel sat at their window and waited to see what would happen. On the dot of six there was a drum roll and the courtyard of the flats was suffused in psychedelic lights: blue, pink, yellow and mauve.

"It's so pretty," moaned Ethel. "Our lights

are boring, they just light the place up." But her voice was drowned out by the sound of Beatles' songs being blasted out. Everyone ran to their windows and flung them open, laughing at all the sound and colour. Soon every single window in the block was open and whole families were hanging out of their windows to see what would happen next.

After ten minutes a young man and a young woman came sailing into the courtyard on the witches' broomsticks, dressed in blue jeans with red T-shirts that had "Broomstick Deliveries" splashed right across them and a picture of a plate of steaming hot food underneath. On their heads they wore bright red and white baseball caps.

So many orders were being shouted from the windows that the Broomstick Delivery people were completely overworked.

That night the phone at Broomstick Services didn't ring once. "We've had it, Mabel," groaned Ethel. "We'll never work again."

"All those people – we thought they were our friends," sniffed Mabel, tears rolling down her plump cheeks. "And we've been dropped like a hot potato just because they're more trendy and are giving away a free Coke."

"We can always go back to dear old Mr Botch and get work moving rubbish," Ethel reminded her.

Mabel groaned, "Well, that's not much to look forward to, is it? I mean, we didn't only do the deliveries for money, let's face it – we did it to be part of the community, to have friends, to help people. Working for Botch is just hard work and no fun."

"We'll have to do it," her sister insisted. "We've got to eat and pay the bills."

"I know that," grumbled Mabel. "But I hate getting up early every day and smelling awful and being filthy."

"So do I," agreed Ethel. "And I agree that the deliveries in the flats were fun – that wasn't like work."

"Oh well, those days have gone, never to return," sighed her sister. "I can see hard times ahead, very hard times."

Over at Jackie's gran's flat, Maud and Gran

and Jackie were watching the display. Ever since she had stopped being a witch Maud had begun to dress in bright red and wear long earrings and have her hair permed, but that evening she managed to look like a witch anyway. Her eyes were gleaming with rage.

"I think we should take advantage of Broomstick Deliveries' generous offer of free delivery and free Coke," declared Maud.

"Maud, you *can't*," said Gran in a shocked voice. "Those people out there stole your sisters' broomsticks and they are trying to take over their business."

"Gran's right," agreed Jackie hotly. "It just wouldn't be right to side with them. Everyone else in the flats may have fallen for Broomstick Deliveries because they're more snappy and up-to-date, but we shouldn't go along with that."

"I am not going along with it, Jackie, as you put it. I am trying to think up a way to demolish the opposition." And with that, Maud flung open the window and called out in her powerful voice, "Over here, over here at number 182, my good man "

"Evening all, lovely evening. Now what can I get you lovely young ladies?"

"Smarmy creature," whispered Gran under her breath.

"Makes me want to throw up," growled Jackie.

"I will have two spring rolls, a portion of sweet-and-sour pork and some chips," Maud told him. "Gran, what about you? Come on, make up your mind, we can't keep this busy young man hanging around."

"It's a pleasure for a lady as lovely as you, love," said the delivery boy.

Jackie got a bit worried. "I hope she doesn't turn him into a frog or something," she muttered, but Maud just smiled and asked Jackie what she wanted. Gran ordered hake and chips and Jackie decided to have a kebab, and he flew away, blowing kisses as he went.

"How can you be so nice to him, Maud?" demanded Jackie.

Maud laughed. "I'm not being nice to him Jackie, I'm just planning my revenge. How dare they steal those broomsticks? Why, one of them belonged to our Grandmother Merlina the Great and the other to our Great Aunt Morgana the Wicked. I might have forsworn witchery but the honour of all witches everywhere and at all times is at stake here and those villains must fail and be seen to fail. Fear not, their hour of glory will be brief, very brief indeed."

Morgana the Wicked

Merlina the Great

"What *are* you planning, Maud?" said Gran.

"Don't you think we should get Mabel and Ethel over?" asked Jackie. "They may be able to help."

"Certainly not," cried Maud, her splendid black eyes flashing. "They're both as silly as rabbits, those two. This task will have to be done by me, Maud, who was once a great witch and the scourge of all who knew her."

"You mean you're going to do this alone?" asked Jackie.

"No," said Maud, *you* are going to help me."

"Me?" yelled Jackie, her eyes growing big with delight. "You mean you'll let me help you with witchcraft?"

"You've always said you want to be a witch, well, now is your chance to ream."

"Can I Gran? Pl*eeease*?"

"It's all right by me," said Gran with a chuckle. "My experience of witches has been very positive. Ever since he married Maud, my son Fred has been a new man."

At that moment there was a knock at the window and there was the young man from Broomstick Deliveries, smiling broadly. Maud smiled back and opened the window.

"Your order, miss: one Chinese, one fish and chips, one kebab and three free Cokes."

"You're so kind and efficient," said Maud sweetly. "So much better than those silly old witches. Now how much do I owe you?"

"Nine-fifty, please love, and, er, I was wondering what you're doing on my night off?"

"I don't know when that is," said Maud in a sugary tone. "But I expect you'll be having lots of nights off soon. There you are, ten pounds and keep the change. Byee, take care, enjoy the rest of the evening." And she slammed the window shut, muttering, "Yes, enjoy the rest of the evening for you won't have many others on dear Grandmother's broomstick!"

The three sat round and picked at their food.

"I'm not hungry," announced Jackie. "I'm too excited."

"Eat up," Maud told her. "We don't want to waste good food and we've got a lot to do tonight."

"What are you planning, Maud?" asked

Gran, beginning to feel a bit alarmed. "I don't want Jackie involved in anything nasty."

"Nothing nasty," Maud assured her as she munched her spring roll. "I will teach Jackie just enough witchcraft to sort out those villains, that's all."

"What are you going to do, Maud?" asked Jackie, as Maud finished her food and bent over an old chest and pulled out her creased witch's costume.

"Huh, I never thought I'd be wearing this again," Maud said as she shook the mothballs out of the long black dress. "I haven't quite decided what I'm going to do, but in this trunk is the *Book of Spells* dear Mother left me. Start reading the section marked 'Revenge', while I *on this dress. For tomorrow we strike!"

Chapter 5

Revenge

The next evening Ethel and Mabel sat miserably by the phone. There wasn't a single call.

"Fine friends we had," moped Ethel. "Not one call in two days. Even our own sister Maud and Jackie and Gran bought food from Broomstick Deliveries last night."

"I know," agreed Mabel gloomily. "I would never have expected it of Maud. And them riding around on Merlina's and Great Aunt Morgana's brooms, too! I mean Maud was always the one who ranted and carried on about witches and their rights."

"Well, she's married to a human now," Ethel reminded her, "but Maud *did* come and fetch us on her broom when we were stranded, so there must be a bit of the witch left in her."

"Well, that may be, but I'm not talking to her until she apologizes."

The witches sat miserably in silence for a moment and then Mabel said, "Do you think, Ethel, that when they stop giving away free Coke they won't be so popular?"

"Who knows?" replied Ethel. "They're so bright and fun-looking. I mean – we don't look so wonderful all in black."

"Mmmmm," nodded her sister. "It is a bit drab. You know when we decided to stop being bad witches and go straight?"

"Yes?" said Ethel.

"Well, we wanted to bring witches up-to-date and stop being so old-fashioned, didn't we?"

"Yes," said Ethel again.

"Well, maybe we can still be witches, but make our outfits more trendy."

"You mean then we might be able to compete with Broomstick Deliveries?"

"Along those lines," said Mabel.

"Well, I'm not going to wear blue jeans and a T-shirt and that's that," Ethel informed her firmly.

"I'd look worse in jeans and a T-shirt than you would," laughed Mabel, "but maybe we could wear sort of trouser suits, you know – baggy trousers and a long top. Mine would be mauve with stars and moons all over it."

"Trousers are a good idea – less draughty on a chilly night. I'll have mine in pink, it's my favourite colour."

"You wear pink and I'll wear mauve then. Let's go and tell Maud about our plan. Oh dear, I forgot – we aren't speaking to her."

Just then there was a tap at the door.

"A customer!" yelled Mabel.

"Yippee," cried Ethel, racing to the door. Their faces fell when they saw Gran, holding a big bowl, steaming hot.

"Can I come in, girls?" asked Gran cheerfully.

"No," said Ethel, sticking her nose in the air.

"I've brought you both a lovely hot supper – your favourite, spaghetti bolognese."

"No, thanks," said Mabel, trying not to lick her lips.

But Gran came in anyway, put the spaghetti

on the table and went into the kitchen to get some bowls. "I know why you two are miffed. You think we didn't stand by you, don't you?"

"We most certainly do! We saw you – you and Maud and Jackie all ordering food from those people and chatting them up."

"It was part of a plan, Maud's plan for revenge. So come on now, eat your tea, because you're going to see something tonight, something spectacular."

"What?" demanded the witches together.

"I don't know, exactly, but Maud is all dressed up in her witch's gear and looking very fierce, and she and Jackie are making spells listed under 'Revenge' in your mother's *Book of Spells*."

Mabel raced to the window and looked out."I can just see her, she's out there under the tree and there's another witch with her!"

"That's Jackie – she's become an apprentice witch."

"And Black Cat, he's out there with them too."

"He ran past me when I came in," smiled Gran. "He knows he's needed."

Mabel rubbed her hands together with glee. "Oh, there's going to be a ruckus tonight! Ooooh, I wonder what they're going to do. Now did someone say something about spaghetti bolognese?"

"I knew Maud hadn't really turned her back on us," grinned Ethel, her mouth full of spaghetti. "Once a witch, always a witch, that's what I say."

Just as they finished eating, the lights came on and the music started. The three of them dashed over to the window and flung it open.

At first nothing happened. It was just like the night before, with Broomstick Deliveries being kept very busy. In the shadows Maud and Jackie and Black Cat were dancing round the big cauldron.

"I bet she's doing one of her '*By toad in ditch and owl in tree*' ones," giggled Mabel. "You'd better watch it, Broomstick Deliveries, you'd better just watch it!"

Suddenly, up in the air, the broomsticks

started to misbehave. They began to wriggle and buck just as the food was about to be delivered. Hot Chinese food and curry, tomato ketchup, chips and ice-cream went all over the people waiting in the windows, all over the delivery people and all over the people watching the scene, below.

Everyone who was watching laughed and laughed, none of them harder than Ethel and Mabel and Gran.

"Good old Maud!" cried Ethel, wiping her eyes.

"She's really showing them," agreed her sister.

The boy and the girl doing the deliveries had to hang on as hard as they could, and no matter how often they tried to land, the brooms just took them faster and faster round the courtyard. The twisting and twirling of the brooms became more and more frantic, and the two up in the air begged to be allowed to land.

Then through a microphone came Maud's voice: "If I let you come down, will you return the brooms to their rightful owners?"

"Anything, anything you say!" they screamed. "Just let us come down, *pleeease* let us come down."

Maud gave the brooms one last whizz and then let the terrified and exhausted pair down. As they landed Maud walked over to them.

"She's going to give them no end of a wigging," said Mabel.

"Glad it isn't us," agreed Ethel. "Come on, we'd better join them and help sort all this out."

When the two witches got to the spot, Maud was exclaiming in a splendid tone, "You two miserable worms, you deserve to be turned into snakes for the way you behaved. Now tell me why you stole the broomsticks of my grandmother the Witch of Witches, Merlina and that of my wicked Great Aunt Morgana?"

"We didn't steal them," cried the boy.

"No, honestly," agreed the girl. "The jobs were advertised in the local paper, we were interviewed by three men and we got the jobs. Wish we hadn't! That was awful."

"What did the three men look like?" asked Mabel.

"Well, they were all middle-aged and one was very tall and thin with glasses," said the boy.

"Yes, and one of them had lots of red hair and the other one was fat and bald."

"Mr Botch!" cried Mabel.

"And Mr Break and Mr Bungle from the sound of it," agreed Ethel.

"They didn't give any names," wept the girl. "We thought it was just a stunt, we didn't mean to cause any hassle."

"You just go home and have a hot bath," said Mabel kindly. "It wasn't your fault, and I'm sorry you had such a rotten night. Come on, Maud and Ethel, let's go and sort this out."

"What about me?" Jackie asked indignantly.

"Oh, all right," said Mabel. "You come too."

So the four of them strode over to the building firm of Botch, Bungle and Break. A curious crowd followed them. When they got there Maud knocked briskly on the door. Mr Botch answered.

"Hello there," he said. "So you got home all right, the other day, did you, Miss Mabel and Miss Ethel?"

Maud's eyes flashed and she stuck her forefinger into Mr Botch's chest.

"Thief, liar, monster!" she cried. "What shall I do to you as punishment?"

"For what?" cried Mr Botch. "What have I done? I was just working a bit late."

"A likely tale," cried Maud, her eyes blazing.

"Now where are your two accomplices, Bungle and Break? Tell me or I'll turn you into a toad."

"No, Maud," interrupted Ethel and Mabel. "Not that!"

"Where are they?" demanded Maud, taking hold of Mr Botch's tie and pushing him against a wall.

"I don't know, really I don't. The firm is in a bit of financial trouble you see and I think Bungle is off trying to raise some money."

"Ah, so now I begin to understand. The firm of Bungle, Botch and Break is in trouble and so you thought you could muscle in on our business," said Mabel. "And all that stuff about the rubbish was just part of a scheme to get your horrid little hands on our broomsticks."

Mr Botch burst into tears.

"All right, I confess but I only did it because I was desperate. The firm of Botch, Bungle and Break is a hundred and fifty years old – I couldn't let it go to the wall! I'm sorry, but I have six children – three at university and the others all need so many things. Please forgive me."

"Worm, iron filings, mouse droppings," yelled Maud. "Forgive you? Never!"

"Excuse me, Maud," interrupted Ethel firmly, "but I think Mabel and I should have some say in all of this."

"Yes," agreed Mabel, "and I think Mr Botch should contact Mr Bungle and Mr Break and get them over here. I don't see why he should take all the blame."

So Mr Botch rang his two partners and reluctantly they joined him in the office.

They sat in a line in front of Maud – Mr Botch all chubby and round, Mr Break long and very thin and Mr Bungle, who was somewhere in the middle.

"Good," said Maud in a silky tone. "Now that I've got you all together what I suggest – dear Mr Botch, Mr Bungle and Mr Break – is that you might like to spend a short period of your lives as mice. I'm sure that Black Cat here would enjoy that. Wouldn't you, pussy?"

Black Cat grinned and waved his tail and walked up and down, nuzzling Maud's legs.

"Oh no, Miss Maud, please don't do that.

Please, please, please, we've all got families. We'll do anything you say but please not mice," the three men pleaded.

"I'm tempted, very tempted. My fingers are itching – I *need* to make a spell," purred Maud.

"Stop it, Maud," cried Ethel firmly. "Just stop, you're scaring them half to death and Mabel and Jackie and I have another idea."

"Oh really, sisters dear? And what is that, pray?"

"What we suggest is that Botch, Bungle and Break take our two new broomsticks and we will keep dear Merlina's and wicked Great Aunt Morgana's and then there will be *two* broomstick businesses – Broomstick Services as before (which will continue to do deliveries) and Broomstick *Removals* run by Mr Botch, Mr Bungle and Mr Break, which will specialize in removals."

"You're soft you two," sneered Maud.

"Maybe," said Mabel. "But we all like Mr Botch and though he did a rotten thing he's not such a bad chap, and when we get to know Mr Break and Mr Bungle, well I expect we'll like them a lot, too."

"You are so kind," cried Mr Botch."I'll do anything you ask. We'll do all the work for the rest of the evening to give you a night off."

"Yes, we'll give you a night off a week,"

said Mr Bungle. "Any time you want, you just ask."

"We owe you ladies a lot," agreed Mr Break. "If it wasn't for you we'd all be mice." At that moment Black Cat let out a disappointed wail.

"Yes, and you've helped us save our business, Miss Ethel and Miss Mabel. We are so grateful to you," declared Mr Bungle.

"And we don't deserve it," sniffed Mr Botch, a tear running down his cheek. "That was a dirty trick I played on you both."

"Well, we modern witches are like that," Ethel told him. "We turn the other cheek. Forgive and forget, that's our motto. Isn't that right, Mabel?"

"Certainly is," agreed her sister.

"Forgive and forget," sneered Maud.

"Some witches you are!"

"Quiet, Maud," Mabel said firmly.

"We're very grateful for all your help but *we* have to settle this." Then, turning to the three men, she continued, "Now the first thing we're going to ask is that you wear colourful suits with stars on to do your delivering, because Ethel and I are brushing up our image a bit."

"Whatever can you mean?"

"You will see tomorrow night, Maud dear. Now thanks for everything but excuse us – Ethel and I have some sewing to do."

"I simply cannot imagine what you mean," sniffed Maud. "And I was looking forward to turning them into mice. I feel quite cheated."

"Come on, Maud, you know that we don't do things like that any more," Ethel reminded her. "So off you go home and tomorrow night you will get a surprise."

The next night everyone was at their windows, waiting to see what would happen. On the dot of seven o'clock, music blared out and four broomsticks swept into the courtyard, with Ethel in a pink trouser suit, Mabel in a star-spangled mauve trouser suit and Mr Botch in red on one broomstick and Mr Break and Mr Bungle on the other one in green. They flew round giving everyone cards, and on them was printed:

BROOMSTICK SERVICES
Wishes to inform its clients
of a new service...

BROOMSTICK REMOVALS
The easiest and quickest
way to transport small
items, no delays in traffic
jams GUARANTEED!

Broomstick Removals turned out to be just as successful as Broomstick Services.

In fact, Broomstick Removals made so much money that soon the building firm of Botch, Bungle and Break were out of their financial difficulties.

"You won't have to fly round in the sky delivering parcels and clearing stuff away now," said Ethel sadly, as she sat drinking a cup of tea with Mr Bungle.

"No," agreed Mr Bungle, looking rather gloomy.

At that moment Mr Botch and Mr Break flew into the courtyard on their broomsticks.

"Miss Ethel was saying that we won't need to go flying around now that the firm is out of difficulties," sighed Mr Bungle.

"I know," said Mr Botch. "But I enjoy it so much, I don't want to give it up."

"Me neither," agreed Mr Break.

"Then we won't give it up," declared Mr Bungle. "Three days a week we'll continue to offer our removal service. Not only for money but also for fun."

"Yippee!" yelled Ethel "That's great news."

"Let's have a Broomstick Services and Broomstick Removals party," suggested Mr Botch. "And invite all our customers."

So the biggest party anyone could remember was held at Hallowe'en in the Town Hall and everyone came dressed as witches and wizards and they all danced and ate and sang. At midnight the Lord Mayor asked for quiet and proposed a toast.

"To Broomstick Services and Broomstick Removals, who serve our community so well."

"To Broomstick Services and Broomstick Removals," cried everyone, and a big cheer went up.

"Well," said Jackie. "Another success story for you modern witches. I can't wait to grow up and join you and start my very own broomstick service!"

The End